This book belongs to:

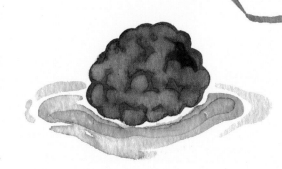

_____

CUENTO
DE LUZ

To Ana Cañizal,
my generous and caring friend.

- Gabriela Keselman -

It's a Gift!

Text © Gabriela Keselman
Illustrations © Nora Hilb
This edition © 2013 Cuento de Luz SL
Calle Claveles 10 | Urb Monteclaro | Pozuelo de Alarcón | 28223 | Madrid | Spain
www.cuentodeluz.com
Title in Spanish: ¡Te lo regalo!
English translation by Jon Brokenbrow

ISBN: 978-84-15784-92-0

Printed by Shanghai Chenxi Printing Co., Ltd. September 2013, print number 1395-2

FSC
www.fsc.org
MIX
Paper from
responsible sources
FSC® C007923

It's a gift!

Gabriela Keselman * Nora Hilb

Little Duck opened his beak and dived into the pool. Since his beak was still open, he swallowed a little bit of water. But he didn't mind. He swam, he splashed, and he sploshed. He even pretended he was a fountain.

Something on the river bank caught his eye. His friend Beaver was covering her head with her paws. She was running between the rushes looking for some shade. Finally, she tried to stick her head in a molehill.

Little Duck thought it was very strange, so he waddled over to her as quickly as his tiny legs would take him. "What's up?" he asked.

"My cap was itchy so I didn't put it on," explained Beaver unhappily. "And now the sun's burning me!"

Little Duck thought about how he could help her. Then he opened his beak and dived into the water again. He swam over and grabbed the nest where he usually took his nap and he gave it to Beaver.

"It's a gift!" he said. "It might tickle a bit, but it'll protect you from the sun."

"Thanks!" said Beaver. "This makes a perfect hat!"

And she laid down in the sunniest meadow,
without a care in the world.

Little Duck was feeling hungry. He took out his favorite sandwich. It was just two pieces of bread on top of each other, but it was his favorite sandwich all the same.

But then a noise distracted him.

He turned around and saw his friend Squirrel searching through her backpack. Squirrel's tummy was mumbling and grumbling.

Squirrel was, too.

Little Duck was worried. "What's up?" he asked.

"I've lost my nuts!" cried Squirrel. "And now I'm hungry."

Little Duck had opened his beak to take the first bite out of his sandwich, but he closed it. "It's a gift!" he said to Squirrel. "I know it's not a nut, but it's my favorite sandwich!"

"Thanks!" said Squirrel. "I've never had a sandwich made of just bread!"

She licked her lips as she worked out where to start.

Little Duck opened his beak again. Now he was going to have a swim. And a splash. And a splosh. And he was going to pretend to be a fountain, but he didn't have time. His friend Bear suddenly appeared, and put his head on his shoulder. And he started to cry.

Little Duck stroked his head. "What's up?" he asked.

"My jar of water tipped over," sobbed Bear, "and now I haven't got anything to drink!"

Little Duck opened and closed his beak a few times. Then he took Bear by the paw and led him down to the pool.

"It's a gift!" he said. "You can drink all of this water."

"Thanks!" said Bear. "I'll drink it all!"

And so he did. He drank and drank until not a single drop was left.

Little Duck decided to take a walk, but he bumped into his friend Mouse.

Mouse was trying to write with the tip of his finger. Then he tried with his whiskers, and finally with his tail.

Little Duck walked up to him, intrigued. "What's up?" he asked.

"I haven't got a pencil to write with," said Mouse, "and I just thought of a really nice poem."

Little Duck had an idea. He plucked a feather out of his chest. "It's a gift!" he said. "You can write with this."

"Thanks!" exclaimed Mouse. "I'll use your feather to write a really great poem!" He dipped the tip of the feather in a squashed blueberry and began to write.

Finally, Little Duck sat down on the river bank. He looked around him.
And he looked at himself. Then he wrinkled up his little beak. And then
he twisted it. Then he shook it from side to side. Tears welled up in
his little eyes, and began to run down his face. It looked like he was
pretending to be a fountain again. But he wasn't pretending this time.

He didn't have a nest for his nap.

He didn't have his bread sandwich.

He didn't have any water to dive in with his beak open.

He didn't even have his feather.

"I haven't got anything!" he wailed.

Suddenly, Beaver, Squirrel, Bear and Mouse appeared. They each gave him a huge hug and said, "Little Duck, what you have is a great big heart!"

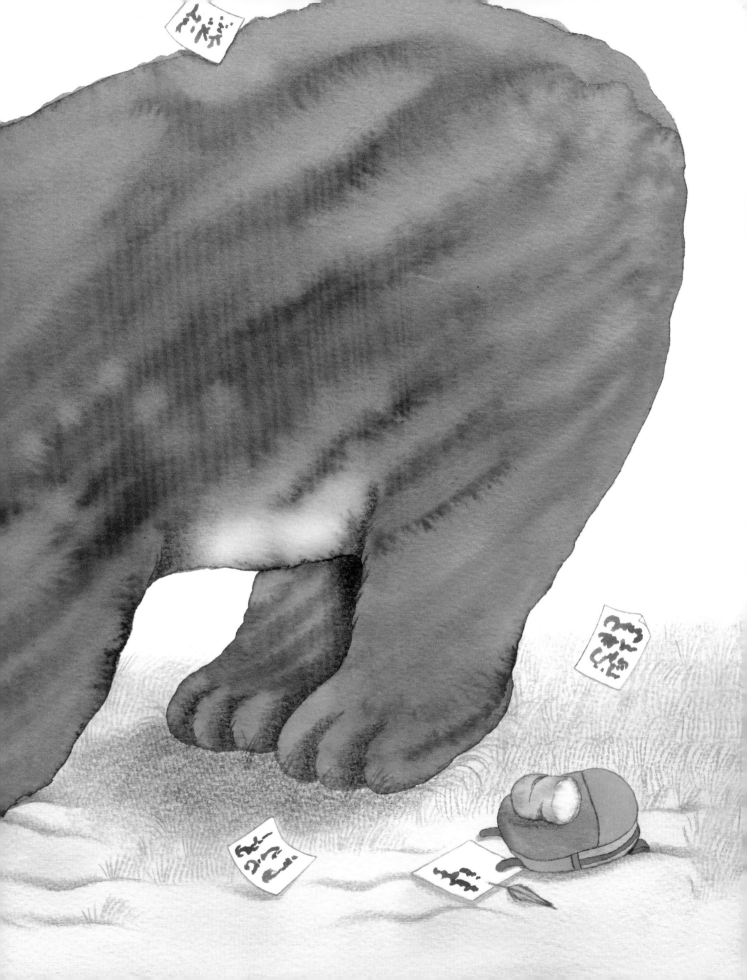

Just then, Little Duck saw his friend Otter. She was running towards him with a bathtub full of water.

"It's my bath time, but I want you to have this!" she said.

Little Duck's smile returned. He opened his beak and he dived in. And *because* he had his beak open, he swallowed a toy frog. But he didn't mind.

He swam, he splashed, and he sploshed.

And he even pretended it was a rainy day.

Just then he saw his old friend Rabbit coming over the hill. He was waving a box of cookies at him.

They were all wrapped up with a big bow!